There once was an okapi named Okapi among lots of racehorses in the barn.

MW00439429

Okapi looked almost like
the other racehorses, and he
always thought he was
one of them.

4

Written by: Amit Sharma
Illustrated by: Anahit Aleksanyan

Dedicated To: Ethan Dhawan
and Sarina Dhawan

INTRO

According to Wikipedia.com, The okapi is a giraffid artiodactylmammal native to the Ituri Rainforest, located in the northeast of the Democratic Republic of the Congo, in Central Africa. Although the okapi bears striped markings reminiscent of zebras, it is most closely related to the giraffe. Today, about 10,000–20,000 remain in the wild and as of 2011, 42 different institutions display them worldwide.

Fun Fact: The okapi's tongue is also long enough for the animal to wash its eyelids and clean its ears (inside and out).

The racehorses always ran on the racetrack, but Okapi never got a chance to run in any races because he was different.

Windracer was the fastest horse in the barn. He was Okapi's friend.

One day Okapi asked Windracer,
"When can I race on the racetrack with all the other horses?"

Windracer looked at Okapi and chuckled, "Eeehehehehe Hahahaha! Oh you are silly Okapi."

"You know you look different. You have stripes my friend. You can't race with the horses. You should go run with the zebras. They have stripes just like you. Eeehehehe, hahaha."

8

Okapi was confused and sad. He ran away from the barn to find the zebras. Okapi ran over hills and valleys for miles and miles. He finally found a herd of zebras drinking water at a lake.

Okapi eagerly ran to the zebras and said, "Hello my fellow zebras! My name is Okapi. I am here to run with you all."

The zebras looked at Okapi and laughed,
"Haa ha haha haha."

Night Dreamer, the leader of the Zebras said to Okapi, "You can't run with the Zebras. You look like a donkey. Go play with the donkeys. Hahahaha."

Okapi was once again confused and sad.
But he ran along the green pastures to find the donkeys.
Okapi ran over hills and valleys for miles and miles.

Okapi finally found a drove of donkeys grazing in the green pastures of Donkeyville. He excitedly said, "Hello fellow donkey friends! My name is Okpai. I am here to play with you all."

The donkeys looked at Okapi and laughed loudly.
"Hehaw Hehaw, Hahaha Hahaha."

Sir Worksalot, the leader of the donkeys said to Okapi,
"What are you doing here? You can't play with the donkeys!
You are different Okapi. You look like a racehorse with stripes.
Hahahaha, go race with the horses buddy."

Okapi was again sad and confused. He ran away as fast as he could. He eventually got tired and thirsty, so he decided to take a rest at a watering hole.

As Okapi drank water from the watering hole, a fox noticed Okapi was looking sad. The fox slowly walked up to him.

The fox asked Okapi, "What is your name? And why are you looking so sad old chap?"

Okapi said, "My name is Okapi. All I ever wanted to do was race with the horses in my barn. But the horses told me I can't run with them because I have stripes and I look different. They said I should run with the zebras.

Okapi continued,
"I went looking for the zebras and when I found the zebras,
they told me I can't run with them because I am different.
The zebras said I look like a donkey.
They told me to go play with the donkeys."

Okapi continued, "So then I went looking for the donkeys. When I found the donkeys, they said I could not play with them either. They said I look like a horse with stripes. They told me to go race with the horses."

Okapi told the fox,
"I am so confused and sad.
I don't know what to do now."

The fox listened carefully to Okapi's problem.
The fox was very wise and smart. He quickly
understood Okapi's problem and suggested
a great solution.

He asked Okapi, "What do you really want to do that makes you happy?" Okapi thought about the question for a minute and said, "Well, I grew up in the barn with all the racehorses. All I ever wanted to do was race with them, like my friend Windracer, he's the race champion in the barn."

25

Mr. Fox said, "Hmmm... I have a solution for you my friend. You should go race with the horses in the barn. You should run faster than you have ever ran before. Show the other horses in the barn that you, Okapi, are the fastest and the winner."

Okapi carefully listened to the fox and realized the sly fox was right. Okapi thanked his wise friend, "Thank you for the great advice Mr. Fox." Okapi was no longer sad or confused. He knew what to do now.

Okapi excitedly galloped back to his barn. He was confident he could run faster than any race horse in the barn. He knew he could even run faster than Windracer.

As Okapi causally strolled back into his stall in the barn, he told all the horses that he was going to race against all of them in tomorrow's race. Some of the horses giggled and chuckled at Okapi. "Ehehehehe, Hahahhaha; Ehehehehe, Hahaha."

The next day was the horse championship race.
All the horses were lined up on the track to start the race.

The whistle was blown to start the race.
The horses were off to a great start.

Okapi was in the race. Okapi could not believe it. His dream was coming true.
He was actually racing with the racehorses from his barn.
Racing is what Okapi always wanted to do. Okapi ran as fast as he could.

Okapi used all the strength in his striped legs.
He was keeping pace with the Champion, Windracer.

It was the final lap of the race.
Okapi powered forward with all his might and energy.

Okapi reached the finish line and beat all the other racehorses.
OKAPI WON THE RACE!!!

Okapi won the race and happily galloped back with the racehorses to his barn. All the horses congratulated Okapi on his win. Okapi was so happy because his dream came true.

19163549R00023

Made in the USA
Middletown, DE
06 April 2015